LITTLE MISS
INVENTOR

Roger Hargreaves

Original concept by
Roger Hargreaves

Written and illustrated by
Adam Hargreaves

EGMONT

Little Miss Inventor was as bright as a button.

In fact she was as bright as two buttons.

Her brain was full of bright ideas.

Bright ideas that she turned into inventions in the shed at the bottom of her garden.

Now, Little Miss Inventor lived in an extraordinary house. A house that she had built herself.

A house on wheels!

How clever was that?

She can move house whenever she feels like it!

Her house was full of her extraordinary inventions.

Extraordinary inventions like the electro-zapper egg boiler which cooked perfectly soft boiled eggs in an instant.

And the brillo-bristle teeth brusher for the perfect smile.

And the super-speedy reader page turner.

Little Miss Inventor reads a lot of books.

And she likes to read them quickly!

But Little Miss Inventor did not only invent things for herself.

She also invented things for her friends.

Things like the line marker that she made for Little Miss Dotty that painted lines. Lines of dots!

Now Little Miss Dotty can leave a trail of dots wherever she goes.

She made a special hat for Mr Chatterbox.

The chatter-natter hat.

Now, Mr Chatterbox can talk to as many people as he wants to at the same time.

And she made a back-pack-snack-attack fridge for Mr Greedy.

For snacks on the go.

Mr Greedy need never worry about getting hungry when he leaves the house.

However, last week Little Miss Inventor had a very testing time.

Normally she has no problem thinking up ideas, but last week she was given a challenge that left her with no idea what to invent.

She had to make a birthday present for Mr Rude.

And she did not have a clue.

So, Little Miss Inventor decided to visit Mr Rude in the hope that this might give her inspiration.

But, oh dear, spending time with Mr Rude was not much fun.

You see Mr Rude's idea of fun was not …
well, it was not fun.

It was not fun at all.

Mr Rude was rude to everybody.

He called Mr Nosey, 'big nose'.

He called Mr Clever, 'clever clogs'.

He called Little Miss Tiny, 'titch'.

And he called the waiter in the café, 'lazy'.

Poor Little Miss Inventor.

What could she invent?

What could she invent for such a horribly rude man?

And then in the middle of the night she woke with an idea.

One of her brightest ideas ever.

Little Miss Inventor set to work the very next morning and she invented a machine that made noises.

But not just any old noises.

It made rude noises.

Think of all the rude noises that you have ever heard and those are the noises that Little Miss Inventor's machine made.

And there were some noises that you have never heard.

Like Mr Impossible's hiccupping, burping all-in-one raspberry!

The machine was hilarious.

And Mr Rude thought it was brilliant.

It was the best birthday present he had ever been given.

But the best thing about Little Miss Inventor's rude machine was that Mr Rude no longer upset everybody.

Now, when he meets people, he makes rude noises and that just makes everybody laugh!